The
Trouble
with Owls

D1101949

The Trouble with Owls

Hilda Offen

HAPPY CAT BOOKS

For Hannah Fairless

Published by
Happy Cat Books
An imprint of Catnip Publishing Ltd.
Islington Business Centre
3-5 Islington High Street
London N1 9LQ

First published 2006
1 3 5 7 9 10 8 6 4 2

A CIP catalogue record for this book is available from
the British Library
ISBN 10: 1 905117 18 3
ISBN 13: 978 1 905117 18 5

Printed in Poland

Chapter 1

The Howletts sat in a row.

"How lucky we are!" said Mr Howlett.

"Indeed, my dear," said Mrs Howlett. "We're very, very lucky!"

"Very, very, very lucky!" said Wendy Howlett.

There was a pause.

"Why are we lucky?" asked Wally.

They turned their heads and stared at him.

"What a silly question!" said Wendy. "We're lucky because we have the Honeybells."

"They're so kind and clever," sighed Mrs Howlett.

"And they just happen to be the most interesting family in the whole world!" said Mr Howlett.

They shifted on their branch and

stared down at the house below.
Light shone from its windows and
spilled onto the lawn.

"Let's show them how much we
appreciate them," said Mr Howlett.
They each took a deep breath and
drew themselves to their full height.

"Tu-whit-tu-whit-tu-WHOOOOO!"
they chorused. "WHOOOOO!"

Inside their cosy house the Honeybells frowned.

"It's those owls again!" said Mr Honeybell. "They're very noisy."

"And nosy!" said Mrs Honeybell. "I get the feeling they're watching us all the time."

"And they're messy, too," said Melissa Honeybell. "They're always dropping things on my head – twigs and beetles' wings and those yukky pellets."

"Why, oh why," said Mrs Honeybell, "did they have to come and live in our tree?"

"I like owls," said Michael.

They turned and stared at him.

"Why?" they cried.

"Oh – I don't know," said Michael. "I think they're interesting, that's all."

"Huh!" snorted Mr Honeybell. "Noisy, nosy and nasty! That's what they are!"

"Tu-whit-tu-whooo!" cried the Howletts in their tree. "Tu-whit-tu-whit-tu-WHOOOOOOOO!"

Chapter 2

Wendy and Wally were learning to fly.

They fluttered from branch to branch while their parents watched.

"Very good, my dears," said Mrs Howlett. "You're making excellent progress."

"You'll soon be ready to master

the two H's – Hooting and Hunting," said Mr Howlett. "I know you've made a start on Hooting, but it needs to be louder. Yes, Hooting and Hunting are next on your list."

"My dearest!" interrupted Mrs Howlett. "Haven't you forgotten the most important H of all?"

Mr Howlett looked blank.

"Honeybells!" cried his wife. "There's Hooting, Hunting and Honeybells!"

Mr Howlett smiled.

"As usual, my dear, you are right," he said. "Indeed, the Honeybells should be first on our study list. Children! Repeat after me – 'Honeybells! Hooting! And Hunting!'"

"Hooray!" cried Wendy and Wally, hopping up and down on their branch. "Honeybells! Hooting! And Hunting!"

"She's so talented!" whispered Mrs Howlett.

"So artistic!" sighed Wendy.

Mrs Honeybell was a hat-maker. She made big hats, little hats, feathered hats and flowery hats and she sold them at Craft Fairs up and down the county.

"I wish I could make hats," said Mrs Howlett.

They stood in a row and stared, entranced by Mrs Honeybell's skills.

"Come!" said Mr Howlett at last. "Time for Hooting Practice. We must give Mr Honeybell a proper welcome when he returns home."

And they flew away to the top of their tree and started to hoot.

Chapter 3

After their practice the Howletts fell asleep; and they slept so soundly they did not hear Melissa and Michael come home from school.

"How was the maths test?" asked Mrs Honeybell as Melissa slouched through the door and slung her rucksack in a corner.

"Awful," said Melissa. "I got two out of ten."

"Oh dear," said her mother. "And what about the cross-country, Michael? Did you do well?"

"No," said Michael, who was covered in mud. "I fell flat on my face. In a puddle. I came last."

"Never mind," said Mrs Honeybell. "Better luck next time."

After they'd had their tea, Mrs Honeybell left Melissa and Michael doing their homework and went into the garden.

"Ed's late," she thought and started pruning a rose-bush.

After a while the gate clicked and there stood Mr Honeybell. He was covered in grease and looked very cross.

"Hallo, dear!" said Mrs Honeybell.

"Did you have a good day?"

"No I did not!" said Mr Honeybell.

"Oh dear," said his wife.

"The train was an hour late," said Mr Honeybell. "They said there was a llama on the line. Then the car broke down on the way home. I've had to walk for miles."

"Oh well," said Mrs Honeybell brightly. "It could be worse."

"No it couldn't!" snapped Mr Honeybell. "I got the sack! It's been the worse day of my life."

And he took a running kick at the watering-can. Unfortunately, the can was full of water and he hurt his toe. He leaped up and down the front path, yelping with pain.

The crash and the yelping woke the Howletts.

"Quick!" cried Mr Howlett. "Mr Honeybell is back – we must greet him."

They hopped out of the nest and lined up on their branch.

"Tu-whit-tu-whooo!" they hooted. "T U - W H I T - T U - W H I T - T U - WHOOOO!"

Mr Honeybell choked with rage. He shook his fist at the Howletts

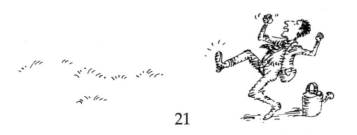

and continued to leap around the path.

"Oh look!" said Mrs Howlett. "How sweet! He's dancing around and waving to us."

"It's nice to be appreciated," said Mr Howlett. "Come on – let's give him an encore!"

And they hooted for all they were worth. Mr Honeybell shook his head in despair and stumbled into the house, slamming the door behind him.

Chapter 4

The days passed and the Howletts noticed that Mr Honeybell no longer went to work.

"He probably wants to see more of us," said Mr Howlett.

"He doesn't want to miss the Hooting," said Wendy.

"I'm not so sure," began Wally, but it was too late; his family was

already taking deep breaths.

"HOOO! HOOOO! HOOOOOOO!" they shrieked.

Mr Honeybell, who was mooching around the garden, looked up.

"See that! He's waving again," said Mrs Howlett.

"I think he's shaking his fist," said Wally.

"Nonsense, dear!" said Mrs Howlett. "Come on – let's give him another hoot. Oh – he's gone indoors."

"Mum! Dad!" said Wally. "I'm tired of Hooting Practice. When are we going to learn Hunting?"

"There's plenty of time for that," said his father. "We've got so much more to learn about the Honeybells."

"In fact," said Mrs Howlett, "tomorrow we're going to set you a Honeybell Test."

"But I'm hungry!" cried Wally. "We've had nothing but moths and beetles for ages!"

No-one answered.

"Look!" cried Mrs Howlett.

On the lawn below Melissa was spreading a pink cloth. She set out four plates, four tumblers and a jug of orange squash. She was joined by Mrs Honeybell and Michael, who were carrying plates of food. They arranged them neatly on the cloth and went indoors again.

"How kind!" said Mr Howlett. "They're offering us a meal."

"Are you sure it's for us?" asked Wally.

"Of course it is," said his mother. "They've set four places, haven't they? Come on!"

The Howletts swooped in formation. They each snatched a tit-bit and flew back to the tree.

Seconds later the Honeybells reappeared, this time bringing Mr Honeybell with them. He was wearing a blindfold and Mrs Honeybell was holding his hand.

When they reached the picnic, Mrs Honeybell whipped off the blindfold and said, "There, dear! This'll cheer you up!"

Mr Honeybell stared. They all stared. What a mess! There were cakes and sandwiches missing, the tumblers had been knocked over and there were crumbs everywhere.

"My fairy-cakes!" cried Mrs Honeybell.

"My egg sandwiches!" moaned Melissa.

"The picnic's ruined!" said Michael.

There was a rustling sound.

Something came bouncing through the branches of the tree and landed at their feet.

"It's a fairy-cake!" cried Melissa.

They looked up.

"Wretched owls!" growled Mr Honeybell.

"Oh – look! They're all waving now!" said Mrs Howlett.

"They're inviting us back again," said Mr Howlett. "Come on – let's finish it up!"

They leaped from their branch and swept down upon the picnic.

The Honeybells scattered in all directions and raced for the back door. Again and again the Howletts swooped. Soon the tablecloth was stripped of everything except the crockery and all the food was neatly arranged along their branch.

"Did you notice how they left us

alone to dine?" asked Mr Howlett. "That was very polite of them."

"And what delicious food!" said Mrs Howlett. "This should last us for days."

The Honeybells cowered inside their house.

"They're greedy. Dirty. Destructive," said Mrs Honeybell.

"That's the trouble with owls," said Mr Honeybell. "And they're a complete waste of space."

There was a short silence.

"But they can turn their heads from the front to the back and see straight behind them!" said Michael. "We can't do that, can we?"

Chapter 5

"Next question!" said Mr Howlett. They were half-way through the Honeybell Test.

"What does Mrs Honeybell make?" asked Mrs Howlett.

"Hats!" said Wally; and Wendy murmured "Beautiful hats!"

Wally yawned. They were staying up all day now so as not to miss a moment of the Honeybells.

"What's Melissa's favourite colour?" asked Mrs Howlett.

"Blue!" said Wendy.

"What's the only thing the Honeybells are scared of?" asked Mr Howlett.

"Cat thieves!" said Wally. "They're scared someone's going to steal their cat."

"And what's their cat's name?" asked Mr Howlett.

"Peter!" shouted Wendy.

"That reminds me, Wally," said Mrs Howlett. "You are on no account to eat Peter, however hungry you are."

"I wasn't going to," said Wally. "He's bigger than me."

"What's the Honeybells' favourite television programme?" continued Mr Howlett.

Wendy and Wally looked blank.

"Never mind," said their mother. "You've done well. And that gives me an idea – why don't we watch television with the Honeybells this evening?"

The Honeybells sat with their backs to the window, watching Singing Superstars.

Mr Honeybell was still grumbling about owls.

"Ghastly creatures!" he snorted. "Not an ounce of sense in the whole of their pathetic little bodies!"

"But, Dad!" protested Michael. "They're so clever! Did you know they can see in the dark?"

"Huh! I'll give 'em 'see in the dark'!" grunted Mr Honeybell.

"Look on the bright side, dear," said Mrs Honeybell, through a mouthful of pins. She was putting the finishing touches to a hat. "Not many people have owls in their garden. Perhaps we should be proud of them."

"Proud?" began Mr Honeybell. "Proud?"

"Nice hat, Mum," said Melissa, hoping to change the subject.

"Thanks, Melissa," said Mrs Honeybell.

She tilted her head to one side and looked at the hat. It was shaped like a large blue saucer and filled with poppies. Clusters of peacock feathers nodded round its brim.

"I think I'll give it a test run on Monday," she said.

Mrs Honeybell always tried out her hats on her friends. She liked hearing their "Oohs!" and "Aahs!" as she entered the room. She knew they were going to like this one.

Behind the Honeybells four pairs of eyes gazed at the flickering

screen. The Howletts couldn't hear a word of the Honeybells' conversation; the music was too loud. Mr Howlett turned to his wife.

"What do you think of the Hooting, my dear?" he asked.

"The Human Hooting? Poor. Very poor," said Mrs Howlett. "No wonder they prefer listening to us."

Chapter 6

It was Monday morning and Wendy was practising her flying.

"Hallo! There's Mrs Honeybell in her new hat," she said to herself. "I'll show her how I loop the loop. She'll like that."

She started to swoop about above Mrs Honeybell's head. Mrs Honeybell failed to notice because the brim of her hat was too wide.

"Help!" thought Wendy as she zig-zagged sideways and lost control. "I'm going to crash!"

She shut her eyes and waited for the Big Bump; but instead she landed on something soft and squashy. She found herself sitting on a bed of poppies. A forest of peacock feathers nodded around her.

"I've landed on Mrs Honeybell's hat!" thought Wendy.

Mrs Honeybell walked on down the path; she was eager to meet her friends for coffee and show off her new creation. So off she went into town, with an owl sitting on her head.

"This is nice!" thought Wendy as the hat swayed from side to side.

She closed her eyes and imagined she was in a cosy nest, with the breeze rocking her gently ... gently ...

And in no time at all she was fast asleep.

Mrs Honeybell noticed she was receiving some rather strange glances; but she thought little of it as she was used to her hats attracting a lot of attention. But then an unusual thing happened; as she drew level with the Animal Rescue Centre a man rushed out and glared at her.

"Madam! You should be ashamed
of yourself!" he snapped.

"I beg your pardon?" said Mrs
Honeybell.

"Our feathered friends need
protecting from people like you!"
said the man, looking crosser than
ever.

Mrs Honeybell thought he must
be talking about the peacock
feathers.

"Don't be silly. They just drop off," she said.

"DROP OFF?" roared the man. "DROP OFF?"

"He must be mad," thought Mrs Honeybell and she walked away as quickly as she could.

The man shook his fist and muttered, "Owl murderer! Stuffing an innocent bird – and all for a hat decoration! Shame on you!"

Mrs Honeybell took no notice as she was out of earshot. She reached the coffee-shop, threw open the door and posed for a moment on the threshold.

Chapter 7

A gasp went round the room.

"Good morning, Mrs Honey –" began the waitress. She stopped as she spotted Wendy and her mouth dropped open. She scurried behind the counter where she started whispering with the waiter.

"Strange!" thought Mrs Honeybell. "I've never had this reaction before!"

She joined her friends at their table.

"Well, girls," she said, twirling round. "What do you think?"

Mrs Parker and Mrs Knox sat and stared.

"You must have some opinion," said Mrs Honeybell. "Don't you like it?"

Mrs Parker gulped.

"Er – it's very nice, Tina," she said.

"Pauline?" asked Mrs Honeybell.

"It's – um – very unusual," said Mrs Knox. She put on her glasses and peered at Wendy.

"What can I get you ladies?" asked the waitress. She had gone pink and was trying not to laugh.

Mrs Honeybell began to feel uneasy. She turned to her friends.

"Monica! Pauline!" she cried. "Whatever's the matter?"

"It's – it's –" began Mrs Knox with a strange quaver in her voice.

She was interrupted by a loud "ZZSHSH!" from the coffee machine.

The noise woke Wendy from her sleep. She opened one eye.

"Aargh!" screamed Mrs Parker. "It's alive!"

Wendy opened the other eye.

"Help!" yelled Mrs Knox, leaping backwards and knocking over her chair.

"Tina!" screamed Mrs Parker. "There's an owl on your hat!"

Chapter 8

Wendy sprang into the air and began to flutter round and round the coffee-shop in a panic. She beat her wings against the windows and knocked over cups and jugs and sugar-bowls. Mrs Honeybell gave a sigh and fainted away on the floor. Fortunately the waitress was a sensible girl and she rushed over and opened the door. Wendy shot

through it like a rocket.

"Where am I?" she wondered and she soared upwards until she was hovering high above the town. In the distance she spotted a familiar landmark.

"Hooray! It's the family tree!" she said and she made a bee-line for home.

She arrived back puffing and panting; her family noticed her feathers were rather ruffled.

"Where have you been?" cried Mr Howlett. "We've been looking everywhere for you."

"Oh – I've been for coffee with Mrs Honeybell," said Wendy casually. She had recovered her composure and was preening her feathers.

"You lucky thing, Wendy!" cried Mrs Howlett. "What was it like?"

"Lovely!" said Wendy. "But I was surprised at how noisy Mrs Honeybell's friends are. I think they tired her out because she fell asleep. That was when I came home."

Mrs Knox and Mrs Parker revived Mrs Honeybell and walked her to her door.

"Look after her – she's had a nasty shock," they told Mr Honeybell.

Mrs Honeybell sank into an armchair and threw her hat on the floor.

"I've changed my mind about owls," she said.

"Have you?" asked Mr Honeybell.

"Yes!" said Mrs Honeybell. "I'm

not proud to have them in the garden after all. They're interfering, sneaky little vermin!"

"Too right," said her husband. "What have they done this time?"

"One of them sat on my hat!" cried Mrs Honeybell. "All the way to town! I'm a laughing stock!"

"Don't say I didn't warn you," said Mr Honeybell.

"And it smashed up the coffee-shop and frightened the customers!" said Mrs Honeybell. "They said it was my owl so I had to pay for the damage. 'My owl' indeed!"

Outside the Howletts began to hoot.

Mr Honeybell looked grim.

"Something," he said, "will have to be done."

Chapter 9

"Mum!" said Wally. "I've got tummy-ache! Please could we go hunting and find some proper food?"

It was the weekend and the Howletts had finished the picnic. Now they were rummaging about in the Honeybells' dustbin.

"We don't need to," said Mr

Howlett, fishing out a used tea-bag. "What do we say in this family?"

"'What's good enough for the Honeybells is good enough for us'!" cried Wendy.

"Exactly!" said her father. "There's plenty of time for hunting.

Tomorrow I'm setting you another Honeybell Test. Now – let's get hooting!"

Wally felt desperate. Stale

sandwiches and tea-bags did not agree with him.

"And Wendy's been for coffee with Mrs Honeybell, too," he thought. "She's bound to get top marks."

Then he had an idea.

Instead of returning with his family to their branch he flew up to the Honeybells' chimney-pot.

He leaned forward. It was amazing! He could hear every word the Honeybells were saying.

"Just listen to that racket!" It was Mr Honeybell. "I don't think I can stand this a moment longer."

"I hate owls!" said Melissa.

"Me too," said her mother. "I think they must be the most obnoxious birds on earth."

"Oh dear!" thought Wally.

Then Michael spoke.

"Owls are the wisest creatures in the animal kingdom," he said. "It says so in my Book of Myths and Legends."

"Nonsense!" said Mrs Honeybell. "That's a myth."

"You're off your rocker, Michael," said Melissa.

"If they're so wise," snapped Mr Honeybell, "Why do they sit around hooting all day? They've got a big shock coming. I bet they're not wise enough to know that."

The Howletts hooted even louder than ever.

WHOOOOOO!

"That's it!" roared Mr Honeybell. "Come on – we're going out!"

At that moment, Wally, who had

been leaning further and further forward to hear what the Honeybells were saying, leaned too far and lost his footing. He toppled over and bumped downwards through the dark, fluttering and kicking. He landed in the fireplace in a shower

of soot, just as the front door slammed shut.

Wally blinked the soot from his eyes and found he was staring straight at Peter the cat.

Wally froze and Peter's hair stood on end. Then Peter gave a wild yowl, rushed into the kitchen and dived through the cat-flap.

"Quick! Wally's fallen down the chimney!" cried Wendy and she darted after him, keen not to miss out on a tour of the house. Mr and Mrs Howlett followed her.

One after the other they dived down the chimney. Wally was more surprised than ever when first

Wendy and then his mother and father landed in the grate beside him amidst an avalanche of soot.

Mr Howlett blinked and looked around.

"Well, now we're here," he said, "Let's make the most of it. Come on, everyone – let's explore!"

Chapter 10

The Honeybells went to the park. They fed the ducks and watched people sailing their model boats. Mr Honeybell and Michael even had a kick-around with some friends. It was a very pleasant afternoon.

"I'm feeling much better for that," said Mr Honeybell as they returned home. Peter padded towards them, meeowing in a pathetic way.

"Yes. I feel calm now," said Mr Honeybell as he unlocked the front door.

"AAARGH!" he bellowed.

"What is it?" asked Mrs Honeybell, peering over his shoulder.

"Oh no! Burglars!" cried Melissa.

The Howletts were still pottering around the kitchen.

"They're home!" said Mr Howlett. "Let's leave them in peace. Through the cat-flap, everyone!"

"It's not burglars!" roared Mr Honeybell. "Look!"

He pointed at four distinct pairs of sooty footprints that led across the carpet from the fireplace.

"Owls!" said Michael.

The house was covered in soot.

The Howletts had poked their beaks into everything. They had walked across the tablecloth, pulled the roses in the bowl to pieces and left black wing-marks up the curtains.

In the kitchen they'd overturned the spaghetti jar, scattered cereal across the floor and dragged the tea-towels off the hook.

They'd gone into the bathroom and left black footprints in the soap, untwirled the toilet roll and knocked over the shampoo bottles which drained onto the tiles with a steady "Drip! Drip! Drip!"

"MUM! MU-U-UM!" wept Melissa, rushing out of her room. "See what they've done to my blue bedspread! And my carpet! And my Sindy doll!"

"Well – what about our room?" cried Mrs Honeybell. "They've eaten my lipstick and they've pecked Dad's ties to pieces. And just look at the pillows!"

"Let's go downstairs and talk this over," said Mr Honeybell with a face like thunder.

They picked their way down the sooty stairs to the living-room. They found a clean patch on the sofa and sat on it.

"Where's Michael?" asked Melissa.

"Upstairs in his room," said her mother. "He must be tidying up."

"We'd better make a start, too," said Mr Honeybell. "And after that, I'm going to fix those owls – once and for all!"

The Howletts gathered on their branch.

"We've learned so much!" said Mrs Howlett.

"What a pretty blue room Melissa has," said Wendy.

"I loved Mrs Honeybell's make-up!" said Mrs Howlett.

"I'd give anything to have socks like Mr Honeybell's," said Mr Howlett. "Those smart diamond patterns – phew!"

Wendy looked round.

"Where's Wally?" she asked.

"Oh no!" said Mrs Howlett. "We must have left him behind!"

Chapter 11

In Michael's bedroom Wally had his beak buried in a book. The book was called "The Wonder of Owls". There were pictures of all sorts of owls – snowy owls, little owls and long-eared owls. There was even a picture of a barn-owl carrying a mouse.

Wally was so engrossed he did not notice Michael come in, take a quick look and close the door softly behind him.

"Hallo!" said Michael and Wally almost jumped out of his feathers. He flew to the top of the wardrobe.

"I'm not going to hurt you," said Michael. "Come on down. You've made rather a mess of my bedroom, haven't you?"

"I'm sorry," said Wally, fluttering back to the table. He and Michael sat and looked at each other.

"Why did you do it?" asked

Michael. "Why did you trash the house?"

"We didn't mean to," said Wally. "We're just interested, that's all."

"You spoiled our picnic," said Michael. "And one of you sat on my Mum's hat and really upset her."

"We like you," said Wally. "We want to learn about you so we can be the same as you."

"But that's silly," said Michael. "You're owls. We're people. You

can't be like us – you can't live on our sort of food, for a start."

"I know," said Wally, as his tummy gave a rumble. "I think it's making me ill."

"And why all the hooting?" asked Michael.

"We thought you'd like it," said Wally. His eyelids began to droop. "We've been staying awake all day so we don't miss anything you do."

"Well – it's driving us mad," said Michael. "Especially my Dad."

"I told the others he looked cross," said Wally. "But they wouldn't listen."

Michael held up the Owl Book.

"You owls are wonderful creatures!" he said. "You can see in the dark!

You're wise! You're beautiful! I wish I could fly like you."

"Do you?" asked Wally.

"Yes – but I know I can't," said Michael.

"I bet you could if you tried," said Wally.

"No! I couldn't. I'm a boy, not a bird," said Michael. "Can't you have a word with your family and get them to start doing owls' things again?"

"I'll try," said Wally.

They could hear Mr Honeybell shouting downstairs.

"I'm afraid my Dad will do something nasty to you," said Michael.

"Michael! Get down here!" yelled Mr Honeybell.

"Coming!" called Michael.

He opened the window and beckoned Wally over.

"You'd better go while the going's good," he said. "What's your name, by the way? Mine's Michael."

"I know," said Wally as he launched himself from the window-sill. "I'm Wally."

Chapter 12

"Mum! Dad! Wendy!" called Wally. "I've got a message from the Honeybells."

The Howletts leaned forward eagerly.

"They want us to know how much they like our hooting!" said Mr Howlett.

"Mrs Honeybell wants me to

help her with her hats!" said Mrs Howlett.

"They want us to come to tea!" said Wendy.

There was a silence.

"No!" said Wally. "They don't like the hooting. They want us to stop. And it was their picnic and we ruined it. And Mrs Honeybell didn't want you to have coffee with her, Wendy. It's all a mistake."

"What?" cried Mr Howlett.

"Rubbish!" shrieked Mrs Howlett.

"You're making it up, Wally," said Wendy. "You're jealous."

"I'm not," said Wally. "Michael told me."

"Oh, Wally!" said Mrs Howlett. "You must have misunderstood." She stroked him gently with her wing. "You are a silly little owlet."

"No, it's true!" cried Wally. "They hate us! Mr Honeybell is going to do something nasty to us!"

"What nonsense, Wally!" said Mr Howlett. "The Honeybells love us!"

"They're so kind to us!" cried Mrs Howlett.

"They're always waving at us!" said Wendy.

"You've got it wrong –" began Wally; but his father tapped him on the beak.

"Not another word!" he said.

First thing on Monday morning Mr Honeybell phoned the council.

He kept his voice down because Melissa and Michael were still in the house.

"We need help!" whispered Mr Honeybell. "We've been over-run by pests."

"What sort of pests?" asked the Pest Control Officer. "Fleas? Cockroaches? Rats?"

"No!" said Mr Honeybell. "Owls."

"Owls?" repeated the Pest Control Officer. "That's not very common."

"Common or not, that's what we've got!" shouted Mr Honeybell. He lowered his voice again. "We're at our wits' end."

There was a silence as the Pest Control Officer flicked through his folder.

"You're in luck," he said at last. "We have one Owl Catcher on our books. I'll send him round."

Chapter 13

While Mr Honeybell was phoning the council, Wally was landing outside Michael's window. He tapped on the glass.

"TU-WHIT-TU-WHOOOOO!" shrieked his family up in their tree.

"No luck, then, Wally?" asked Michael, opening the window.

"No," said Wally. "I'm really sorry.

They won't listen to me."

"I've got to go to school in a minute," said Michael. "But please be careful, Wally. I think my Dad's planning something. And whatever it is –"

"It's bad news for owls?" said Wally.

"Right," said Michael.

That afternoon Mr and Mrs Honeybell went to meet the Owl Catcher. He had parked his van round the corner so as not to alert the Howletts and was unloading his equipment.

"We're going into town," said Mr Honeybell. "Use whatever method you like. Just make sure they're gone by the time we come back."

The Owl Catcher tip-toed down the road and up the Honeybells' front path.

"Look, my dear!" said Mr Howlett to his wife. "A friend of the Honeybells has arrived."

"What's he doing?" asked Mrs Howlett.

They watched as the Owl Catcher prowled round the house, peering through the windows. Then he approached the washing-line and

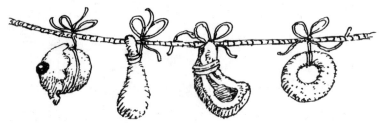

produced a variety of snacks from his rucksack. There was an iced bun, a chicken leg, a lamb chop and a doughnut, each with a length of string attached. The Owl Catcher proceeded to tie each item of food to the washing line. Then he stepped back and admired his handiwork.

"The Honeybells have ordered a take-away for us!" said Mr Howlett. "How kind!"

"No! No!" cried Wally. "It's a trap!"

They turned on him.

"Don't be so silly," said Wendy.

"And suspicious!" said Mrs Howlett.

"It would be ungrateful to refuse it," said Mr Howlett. "And you're going to have some, Wally, like it or not."

They were so busy glaring at Wally they did not notice the Owl Catcher ducking behind a lilac bush next to the washing-line. In his hand he held a huge net.

Chapter 14

It was at that moment that Michael came home from school. It was cross-country again and he was so far behind he'd decided to give up and come home early.

He spotted the Owl Catcher's van and raced towards the gate.

He took in the situation at a glance – the food on the line, the

Howletts poised on their branch and the Owl Catcher crouched behind the lilac with his net dangling over one shoulder.

"I must do something – quickly!" thought Michael.

He spotted his mother's pruning shears lying in the rose-bed. He seized them and tip-toed up behind the Owl Catcher.

"Snip! Snip! Snip!"

Quietly but firmly he cut through the Owl Catcher's net.

Not a moment too soon! With a wild hoot the Howletts launched themselves into the air.

They swooped downwards. They each snatched a tit-bit from the line and –

"GOTCHA!"

Out leaped the Owl Catcher, net at the ready. Into the net flew the Howletts – and ...... out they flew again, through the other end! They were so intent on the food they hardly noticed the net.

The Owl Catcher was speechless. He looked at his net, turned round and saw Michael, who had dropped the shears and was getting ready to run.

"Come here, you!" shouted the Owl Catcher and he seized his second-to-largest net.

The shout alerted the Howletts, who were about to tuck into their snacks.

"Look! The Take-Away Man is chasing Michael!" cried Mrs Howlett.

"He's caught him in a net!" shouted Wendy.

"To the rescue!" shrieked Mr Howlett; and they abandoned their meal and swooped on the Owl

Catcher in a flurry of beating wings. Again and again they flew in to the attack.

"Help!" cried the Owl Catcher and he dropped his net and raced off down the path.

Michael disentangled himself and looked at Wally, who was perched on the washing-line.

"I warned you, Wally," he said.

"I know," said Wally. He looked up at his family, who were already back on their branch, tucking in to their take-away.

"They just won't listen," he said.

Chapter 15

Mr and Mrs Honeybell strolled back from the shops.

"Well, his van's gone," said Mr Honeybell. "It must all be over."

Mrs Honeybell clutched her husband's arm.

"Listen!" she said.

The sound was unmistakeable. It came drifting towards them on the afternoon air – a distinct "Tu-whit-tu-whit-tu-whooo!"

"I don't believe it!" yelled Mr Honeybell and he dashed up the path into the house, while high above him the Howletts hooted a greeting.

Mr Honeybell grabbed the phone.

"You – Owl Catcher!" he roared.

"What happened?"

"You may well ask!" replied the Owl Catcher.

"I am asking!" shouted Mr Honeybell. "The owls are still here!"

"And there they can stay, as far as I'm concerned, mate!" said the Owl Catcher. "Your owls are mad. Stark, staring mad. They attacked me – I could have you up in court!"

"They're not my owls!" screamed Mr Honeybell.

"Well, I'm not coming back," said the Owl Catcher. "Send my nets round to the Council Offices, will you?"

Mr Honeybell banged down the phone in disgust, just as Melissa arrived home from school. A second later, Michael appeared.

"You can say goodbye to those owls," said Mr Honeybell.

"Why?" asked Michael.

"Because their tree's a goner," said Mr Honeybell. "Tomorrow I'm going to cut it down."

Chapter 16

Wally woke the next morning feeling fed up. The night before, he and Wendy had taken the new Honeybell Test; they'd been neck and neck until the final question.

"What do the Honeybells think of us?" asked Mr Howlett.

"They hate us," said Wally truthfully. "All except Michael."

"Wrong!" said his father. "Wendy?"

"They love us to bits!" said Wendy.

So Wendy had won.

As Wally gazed out of the nest he gradually became aware of the sound of twigs snapping below him. Then, to his surprise, Michael's face appeared.

"Hallo, Michael," said Wally as the rest of his family woke up. "What are you doing here?"

"I've come to warn you!" said
Michael, his face rather pale. He
had no head for heights. "My
Dad's going to chop down your
tree."

"My dear child!" said Mr Howlett.
"You must be mistaken."

All the Howletts hopped out of the
nest and sat on the branch, looking
at Michael.

"Your family loves us!" said Mrs Howlett.

"No, they hate you," said Michael.

"I'm afraid you're a bit muddled, Michael," said Mr Howlett. "Our Wally's just the same."

At that moment Mr Honeybell strode across the lawn, followed by Mrs Honeybell and Melissa. He was waving a chain-saw.

"Now you're for it, you little monsters!" he yelled.

The Howletts looked this way and that, but there was no-one else around; Mr Honeybell was definitely addressing them.

Their faces fell. A shudder passed along the row, followed by a deep, deep sigh.

"Wally," said Mr Howlett slowly, looking very sad. "I think you may have been right all along."

"ZZZZ!" went the chain-saw.

"They really hate us!" cried Mrs Howlett.

"Boo-hoo-tu-whit-boo-hoo!" wept Wendy.

Mr Honeybell applied the saw to the tree-trunk.

"But I like you!" said Michael and he started shouting "Rights for Owls! Rights for Owls!" at the top of his voice.

Luckily for Michael, Mrs Honeybell spotted him. She yelled

"Switch it off!" in her husband's ear. Mr Honeybell did as he was told and looked up.

"Rights for Owls!" yelled Michael.

"Michael!" roared Mr Honeybell. "Come down here at once!"

Michael took no notice.

"Rights for Owls!" he screamed.

Chapter 17

Mr Honeybell threw the chain-saw into a bush and leaped at the tree; he was soon half-way up and climbing fast, while above him Michael went on shouting "Rights for Owls!"

The wind began to rise.

"Your father's got no head for heights, Melissa," said Mrs Honeybell.

"Neither has Michael. I'd better go after them."

And she hauled herself up into the tree.

Michael's shouts began to attract the attention of passers-by. At first they watched from the gate, but gradually they drifted into the garden. There were some girls from Melissa's class, their teacher, Miss Emsworth, a postman, some joggers and the man from the Animal Rescue Centre.

"What's your mother doing up the tree?" asked Miss Emsworth.

"She's gone to rescue my father," said Melissa. "And he's gone to get my brother down."

By now the wind was gusting harder than ever; it seized Michael's voice and whirled it away.

"What's he shouting?" asked the postman. "Is it 'Fry the Fowls'?"

"Sounds like 'Dry the Towels' to me," said one of the joggers.

The Animal Rescue man was staring intently at the tree.

"There are four owls up there!" he cried.

"Oh! How wonderful!" said Miss Emsworth. "I love owls – we're doing a project on them next week."

"They're our owls," said Melissa. She thought it best not to reveal the real reason for the Honeybells' climb. "My brother's gone to talk to them."

"Remarkable!" said the man from

the Animal Rescue Centre. "What a family!"

Someone phoned the local paper and soon the crowd was joined by a reporter and a photographer; a passing policeman dropped in, too.

"Tell me," said the reporter, looking excited. "How long has your brother spoken Owl? Is it on the National Curriculum?"

Chapter 18

"Now, look here, Michael! Come down at once!" puffed Mr Honeybell, scrambling onto the branch next to his son.

"No!" said Michael.

Mrs Honeybell clambered up beside them. She noticed they had both turned green and were clinging to the branch for dear life.

"Wretched birds!" said Mr Honeybell to the Howletts. "You've made our lives a misery!"

The Howletts looked astonished.

"How can that be?" asked Mr Howlett. "We admire you! We want to be just like you!"

"You ruined our picnic! You sat on my hat! You messed up the house!" gasped Mrs Honeybell, who was now looking rather green herself.

"You stay up all day and do that horrible hooting!" groaned Mr Honeybell.

"This is ridiculous!" cried Mr Howlett. "Yesterday we rescued your son from a man with a net. Aren't you grateful?"

"Grateful?" repeated Mr Honeybell. "You're living in fantasy land – my son was at school. And that man was an Owl Catcher. I asked him round to get rid of you lot."

The Howletts looked offended and hopped further along the branch.

"And what, pray, was he going to do with us?" asked Mrs Howlett.

"I don't know and I don't care," muttered Mr Honeybell. "Boil you in oil, I hope."

The Howletts whispered among themselves.

"I don't like the Honeybells any more," said Mrs Howlett.

"They're horrible!" said Wendy.

"Mean and cruel!" said Mr Howlett.

They were interrupted by Michael, who gave a shout.

"Look!" he cried, pointing at the house. "It's a Cat Thief! He's got Peter!"

Chapter 19

Sure enough, a sinister-looking person was sneaking out of the Honeybells' house. He wore a mask and a crash helmet and carried a wriggling sack. The Honeybells waved frantically to the crowd and pointed at the thief; but the crowd just waved back.

"Please, Howletts – do something!" cried Mr Honeybell.

Mr Howlett looked huffy and turned away.

"Just now you were going to have us boiled in oil", he said.

"And you were going to cut down our tree," added Mrs Howlett. "Why should we help you?"

"Please!" begged Michael. The Cat Thief was getting away.

Then Wally spoke. "Well – if no-one else is going, I'll go by myself," he said and he dived off the branch.

His family was stung into action. "After him!" cried Mr Howlett.

The thief was caught unawares by the fury of the attack. He fell to the ground and the sack burst open. Out leaped Peter, followed by a cascade of Mrs Honeybell's best hats. The thief's crash helmet rolled off and the Howletts tugged at his hair and pecked him on the nose.

"Ow! Stoppit!" he yelled.

At last the crowd noticed what was happening.

"What's your game, then?" said the policeman and he grasped the thief by the collar and ripped off his mask.

"Well, really!" gasped Mr Honeybell, peering down from the swaying tree. "It's the Owl Catcher!"

The Howletts flew up to the porch roof where they had a ring-side seat.

"You try living on what I'm paid, mate," they heard the Owl Catcher grumble. "I have to have a side-line."

"Pipe down!" said the policeman. He spoke into his radio.

"Send me a squad car!" he said. "And a fire-engine! There are some people here trapped up a tree."

The Howletts watched as the fire-engine tore up the road and the firemen ran into the garden with their longest ladder. They brought the Honeybells down one by one. The reporter was delighted and the photographer snapped away like mad.

"You're not publishing those!" cried Mrs Honeybell as she descended the ladder, slung over the shoulder of a burly fireman.

"You've got to give us something," said the reporter. "What about a group photo of you and the owls?"

"What do you say, Howletts?" asked Michael. "You are the heroes, after all."

"Oh – alright! Just this once," said the Howletts and they flew down from the porch.

Mrs Honeybell put on one of her hats and Mrs Howlett sat on it. The other Howletts arranged themselves on the Honeybells' heads and the photographer snapped away to his heart's content.

"What's it like being friends with a family of owls?" asked the reporter.

"Alright," said Mr Honeybell, through gritted teeth.

"Very nice," said Mrs Honeybell.

"Lovely!" said Melissa.

"It's the best thing in the world!" said Michael.

Chapter 20

The Howletts sat in their tree and discussed the Honeybells.

"They're not very clever and they can't fly," said Mr Howlett.

"They can't see in the dark," said Mrs Howlett.

"It was nasty of them to bring in the Owl Catcher," said Wendy.

"Michael's nice," said Wally.

"Nice or not," said his father, "He has no head for heights. Neither do his parents."

The Howletts decided to stop studying the Honeybells and to go back to being proper owls again. Wendy and Wally even learned to hunt. They didn't give up the hooting, but they made sure they only did it at night, far away in the woods.

The Honeybells did rather well out of the newspaper article. Mr Honeybell was offered a job at the Animal Rescue Centre and hundreds of orders flooded in for Mrs Honeybell's hats. Miss Emsworth asked if she could bring the children round to study the Howletts and Melissa became the most popular girl in the class.

As for Michael, he just felt happy that the Howletts were safe. He and Wally grew to be very good

friends and they often met up to read the Owl Book or watch a video together. So things evened out; for while the Howletts liked the Honeybells a lot less, the Honeybells liked the Howletts a whole lot more.

The Honeybells sat together on the sofa, watching a programme about owls.

"Aren't we lucky?" said Mr
Honeybell.

"Very lucky, dear," said Mrs Honeybell.

"Very, very, very lucky!" said Melissa.

"Why are we lucky?" asked Michael.
They turned and stared at him.

"Because of the Howletts, of course!"
said Mr Honeybell.

"The most interesting family of

owls in the world!" added Mrs Honeybell.

"Tu-whit-tu-whoooo!" called the Howletts, far away in the shadowy woods.

"And they live here!" cried Melissa. "In our garden! Up our tree! "